D0810198

Jip and Janneke

www.queridokinderboeken.nl
www.annie-mg.com
www.anniemgschmidt.nl
www.fiepwestendorp.nl

Original title: *Jip en Janneke* (deel 1: *Poppejans gaat varen
en andere verhalen*)

Eerste druk, 2008; tweede druk, 2010; derde druk, 2011

Cover Pauline Hoogweg
Coverillustration Fiep Westendorp

ISBN 978 90 451 0614 4 / NUR 281

Annie M.G. Schmidt

Jip and Janneke

Illustrated by Fiep Westendorp

Translated by David Colmer

Amsterdam Antwerpen
Em. Querido's Uitgeverij BV
2011

Contents

A note on pronunciation

The Dutch name Jip is pronounced 'Yip'.

Janneke is a little more difficult. It might be easiest to think of as 'Yannicka', with the 'a' as in 'father' and a firm stress on the first syllable.

Jip and Janneke play together

Jip walked around the garden and he was *so* bored.
But look, he's spotted something. A hole in the
hedge. *What's on the other side of the hedge?* Jip
wondered. *A palace? A gate? A knight in armour?* He
sat down on the ground and looked through the
hole.

And what did he see? A little nose. And a little
mouth. And two blue eyes. It was a girl. A little girl
who was exactly the same size as Jip.

'Who are you?' Jip asked.

'Janneke,' the girl answered. 'I live here.'

'You didn't live here yesterday,' said Jip.

'I live here today,' said Janneke. 'Are you coming
to play?'

'I'll crawl through the hole,' said Jip.

He pushed his head through the hole first. And

then one arm. And then the other arm. And then he got stuck. Janneke pulled one arm. And then she pulled the other arm. But it didn't help. Jip was stuck. And Jip started to cry. And then he screamed.

Jip's father came running up in one garden. And Janneke's father came running up in the other garden. And together they helped Jip back through the hole.

'So, Jip,' his father said, 'now you've got a little friend next door. But you have to go out the front door like a good boy, and then in through Janneke's front door. And then you can play together.'

And that's what they did. Jip and Janneke played together. One day they played in Jip's garden. And the next day they played in Janneke's garden. They played mummies and daddies.

Jip's got
a ponytail

Jip is at the barber's. *Snip, snip*, go the scissors. And Jip says, 'Ow!'

'I'm not hurting you,' says the barber. 'How old are you anyway? I didn't even touch you.'

Snip, snip, go the scissors. And Jip hates it. He just hates it. He keeps shouting, 'Ow, ow!'

'Just a little bit more,' says the barber.

But Jip shouts 'Ow!' one more time. He jumps up and runs out of the shop wearing the white barber's cape.

'Hey, where are you going?' the barber shouts. 'You're not finished yet! Just a little longer!'

But Jip has had enough. He runs very fast. And the barber runs very fast after him. But Jip is faster. He's almost home and the barber shrugs and gives up.

9

Jip sits down by the side of the road. He is still wearing the white barber's cape. He's crying because he was so scared.

Here comes Janneke. She sees Jip sitting there. And she starts laughing. She can't help it. 'You look really silly,' she says.

Jip looks up and stops crying.

'You've got a ponytail on top of your head,' says Janneke. And she snorts with laughter. 'You've got a ponytail and you're wearing a serviette.'

And it's true. Jip is almost completely bald, but there is a tuft of hair left on the top of his head. Just like a little ponytail.

Janneke laughs so much it makes Jip angry. 'I'm not going back to the barber's,' he says.

'Then you'll have to walk around with a ponytail for the rest of your life,' Janneke says. 'Jip's got a ponytail, Jip's got a ponytail!'

That really is horrible. Having Janneke laugh at him! That's too much. Jip gets up very slowly and very slowly he walks back to the barber's. 'The ponytail has to come off,' he says.

'I told you that already!' grumbles the barber. 'You ran off before I was finished.' And Jip has to get back on the chair.

Snip, snip, go the scissors.

'There,' says the barber. 'Now it's done. Was it really that bad?'

Jip smiles. The barber undoes the white cape

and Jip is back out on the street.

'My ponytail's gone,' he says to Janneke.

'I can see that,' says Janneke. 'It looked really, really silly.'

And then they play marbles.

Dolly-Dee is sick

What's wrong with Dolly-Dee? She is so sick!

'I'll call the doctor,' says Dolly-Dee's mother. And she grabs the tassel on the end of the curtain cord and shouts, 'Hello?'

'Hello,' says the doctor. He's over at the other curtain.

'Doctor, doctor, come quickly. Dolly-Dee is sick.'

'I'm on my way,' says the doctor. And here he is. His coat is dragging over the floor and his hat is resting on his nose and he's got a wooden spoon in one hand.

'Well, well,' says the doctor. 'I'll just examine her.' And he whacks Dolly-Dee on the head with the wooden spoon.

'No, doctor,' the doll's mother shouts, 'don't do that.'

'This child has a fever,' says the doctor. 'She needs to soak in hot suds.'

'You don't soak in hot suds if you've got a fever,' says Dolly-Dee's mother.

'Listen,' shouts the doctor, 'if you know so much about it, you should be the doctor.' And he grabs Dolly-Dee's leg. The little girl's mother grabs her other leg and they both pull hard. And they scream and they yell.

Janneke's mother rushes in and says, 'What's this? A doctor and a mummy pulling the child apart? I've never seen anything like it, ever.'

'Yes, but he...' says Janneke.

'Yes, but she...' says Jip.

'You can both have a cup of hot chocolate and a biscuit,' says the real mother, 'and you can put

Dolly-Dee back to bed and tuck her in, and then she'll get better by herself.'

They lay Dolly-Dee in her bed and she closes her eyes and thinks, *Thank goodness I've got a grandmother too.*

Apples for Grandpa

'Here's a basket of apples for you to take to Grandpa,' says Jip's mother. 'Carry the basket between you and give my love to Grandpa.'

Jip and Janneke walk along the road with the basket and after a while Jip says, 'There are red apples and green ones.'

'Yes,' says Janneke, 'the green ones taste better.'

'No, they don't,' Jip says, 'the red ones taste better.'

'Let's check,' says Janneke. They put down the basket and Janneke bites into a red apple. Jip bites into a green apple.

'This one tastes better,' says Jip.

'No, this one tastes better,' says Janneke.

Not all red apples taste the same.

'This one looks good. And so does this one,' says Jip.

'And that one,' says Janneke. They sit down on

the side of the road and soon they've tried all of the apples by biting a little piece out of each apple. You can see the teeth marks.

'This is terrible,' says Jip.

'Your grandpa is going to be really angry,' says Janneke.

They pick up the basket again and walk on sadly to Grandpa's house.

'Mother sends her love,' says Jip.

'And here's a basket of apples,' says Janneke.

'But they've all got bites out of them,' says Jip.

'We tried them,' says Janneke. And they both look very, very frightened.

'Really,' says Grandpa, 'bites out of all of them? I bet that makes them taste a lot better. You know what, why don't we all eat one up?"

And that's what they do.

But later, when Jip tells Mother, she says, 'Grandpa is too kind for his own good.'

Do you think that's true?

The baby looks like a piglet

'I've got a new cousin,' says Janneke. 'Do you want to come and have a look?'

'Where is she?' Jip asks.

'At her house,' says Janneke. 'She's brand-new. She's really small.'

'As small as Dolly-Dee?' asks Jip.

'Smaller,' says Janneke. And together they go to the cousin's house.

'This is my Aunty Kate,' says Janneke. 'You can call her Aunty Kate too, Jip.'

'You have to be very quiet,' says Aunty Kate. 'You have to walk on your tiptoes. The baby is asleep.'

Jip and Janneke tiptoe into the room. The baby is lying in its cradle. A cradle with curtains. Very gently they slide back the curtains.

'Oh, she's so little,' says Jip.

'Tiny,' Janneke sighs.

But then the baby wakes up. It cries. It cries very loudly.

'Why is she crying like that?' Janneke asks. 'Dolly-Dee never cries.'

'She's crying because she's hungry,' says Aunty Kate.

'She looks just like the piglets,' Jip says. 'Farmer Jansen's piglets. They don't have any hair either.'

'Would you like to have a little baby at home, Jip,' asks Aunty Kate. 'Wouldn't you like to have a little sister?'

'No,' Jip says. 'I'd rather have a real piglet. Can she play yet?'

But no, the baby can't play yet. She's too small.

Aunty Kate sends Jip and Janneke out of the room.

'I think she's boring,' says Jip.

'I don't,' says Janneke. 'She's cute. You haven't even got a cousin.'

'Mother,' Jip shouts, 'have I got a cousin?'

'Of course you do,' Mother says. 'There's Minnie in Amersfoort. She's six. She's a cousin.'

'See,' says Jip. 'I've got a cousin. She's six. She doesn't look like a piglet.'

And now Janneke's angry and stomps off.

'Go over and talk to her in a minute,' says Mother. 'And tell her you think it's a cute little piglet.'

And Jip does that. And by afternoon everything is all right again.

A bite each

There's Janneke's head poking around the door.
'I'm going out to play,' she says. 'You coming?'
   'I'm not allowed yet,' Jip moans. 'I've got six
pieces of bread left to eat.'
   'What's on it?' asks Janneke.
   'Jam,' says Jip. 'Chocolate jam.'
   'I'll eat two,' Janneke says, 'and you can eat two.
And then they'll be finished.'
   They both eat two and look, there are still two
pieces left.
   'A bite each,' says Janneke, and after they've both
had a bite, there is just one piece left.
   'I don't want any more,' says Janneke.
   'Me neither,' says Jip.
   'Has Bear had anything to eat?' asks Janneke.
   'Yes,' says Jip, 'he's already had four sandwiches.'
   'Do you think he'd like another little piece?'
   And together they give Bear a piece of bread.

But Bear keeps his mouth clamped shut.

'See,' says Jip. 'He's full too.'

'He has to!' Janneke says. 'He has to get big and strong.'

And they try again.

'Now it's finished,' says Jip. And he's right, the piece of bread is gone, there are only crumbs left.

'Let's go and play outside,' says Janneke.

And after they've gone outside, Bear is all alone at the table. He's brown and sticky from the chocolate jam. But he looks very proud, because he's had four whole sandwiches. And a little piece too!

Rice-pudding dog

Jip and Janneke walk hand in hand down the road. They're going to the farm. But when they get to the gate they stop.

'Look,' Jip says.

'A cow!' Janneke says.

'No,' Jip says, 'it's a dog. A very big dog. I'm not scared of it.'

'Neither am I,' Janneke says.

But then the dog comes bounding over to Jip and Janneke. They both scream at the tops of their voices and run off. But the dog runs a lot faster.

'Mother!' Jip shouts.

'Father!' Janneke screams.

But they're so far from home that Mother and Father can't hear them.

Luckily the farmer comes along. He grabs the dog and says, 'Sit!'

'This is Hector,' he tells Jip and Janneke. 'He's a

good boy. He won't hurt you. You can pat him.'

Jip and Janneke stick out their hands and pat the dog. And the dog wags his tail.

'He's so big,' says Jip.

'And cute,' says Janneke. 'He's a rice-pudding dog. White with black spots. Just like rice pudding with raisins.'

Then the farmer puts Jip and Janneke on Hector's back. He lets them go for a ride and it's great fun. Because that's not the kind of thing that happens every day, going for a horsey ride on a rice-pudding dog.

Janneke is a bit fluey

Janneke isn't feeling very well.

'Can I go and see her?' asks Jip.

'No,' his mother says. 'Janneke is a bit fluey.'

'How fluey?' asks Jip. 'This fluey? Or this fluey?'

'About this fluey,' says Mother. 'You'll just have to play by yourself today, and tomorrow as well.'

That's miserable. Jip doesn't know what to do. His top is broken. And Bear doesn't want to play with him, he only wants to sleep.

'I'll stand on my head,' Jip says. And he does. But he keeps falling over.

Finally Jip goes outside. There's Janneke's house. But he doesn't dare to go inside. Someone is standing at the window. Look, it's Janneke's mother. And Janneke is there too, with a scarf around her neck. A woollen scarf.

'Hi,' says Jip.

'Hi,' says Janneke. But she's so far away. The window is so high up.

Then Jip sees the rubbish bin. He drags it over to the window. And then he climbs on top of it. Now he can look inside. And he can press his nose against the glass.

Janneke presses her nose against the glass too. Two noses pressed against each other, with the window in between.

'Hi,' says Jip.

'Hi,' says Janneke. And then she has to go back to bed.

And Jip goes home and calls out, 'I played with Janneke anyway.'

'What?' says Mother, 'you naughty boy!'

'Through the window,' says Jip.

And then his mother smiles again.

Jip hates tea

Janneke is better again. But Mother has said, 'You're still not allowed to go outside.'

'Where shall we play then?' asks Jip.

'In the kitchen,' says Janneke.

'Not in the kitchen,' says Mother. 'You'll just get in the way. Go up to the attic and play there.'

It's fun in the attic. You only have to lean two planks against the wall and you've made a house.

'We'll play mummies and daddies,' says Janneke.

'No,' Jip says, 'I don't want to play with dolls anymore.'

'Not even your bear?' asks Janneke.

'He's not a doll, he's just Bear.'

'Then we'll play ladies and gentlemen,' Janneke says. 'Would you like to come to afternoon tea, sir?'

'Yes, please,' says Jip.

'Would you like a cup of tea, sir?'

'No,' Jip says, 'I hate tea.'

'Goodness,' Janneke says, 'a gentleman would never say that. A gentleman sits down politely and politely drinks his tea.'

'Then I don't want to be a gentleman, ever,' Jip says.

'What do you want to be?'

'A lawyer,' Jip says. 'I want to be a lawyer and smoke a pipe.'

'But lawyers aren't allowed to say "I hate tea" either.'

'Yes, they are,' Jip says. 'Lawyers are allowed to say that.'

'They're not,' says Janneke.

'They are,' says Jip.

'I'll go ask Mother,' Janneke says.

And Mother says, 'When Jip's a lawyer, he'll be a grown-up. And when Jip's a grown-up, he'll like tea.'

'See?' says Janneke.

But it all sounds very strange to Jip. He has to think about it first. And he takes down the house in the attic. 'I don't want to play ladies and gentlemen anymore,' he says. 'I've brought my marbles.'

And then they have a fun game of marbles in the great big attic.

Cutting out pictures

Oh, it's such a wet day! It's so wet! It's much too rainy to play outside.

Jip and Janneke sat on the windowsill for a while looking out. But no one came past. Just a little dog.

Then they looked at pictures. And now they've finished all of the picture books. And it's raining and raining.

'Here are two pairs of scissors,' says Jip's mother. 'One each. You can have this book to cut pictures out of, and this one too, and that one too. Three books to cut pictures out of.'

Now they've got something fun to do. There are lots of pictures of cars and lots of pictures of beautiful ladies. They cut out all the pictures they can find and after a while there aren't any left.

'Finished,' says Janneke. 'There's nothing left to cut out. Are there any more books?'

Jip looks at the bookcase. On the bottom shelf

there are books with lots of beautiful coloured
pictures. 'These would be all right,' says Jip.
'They're at the bottom. Nobody ever looks at them.
Here, you cut out from this book, and I'll take that
one.'

They concentrate so hard their tongues are
sticking out. And they don't even notice someone
coming in.

'Hey! What are you doing?' a voice shouts.

Jip and Janneke drop their scissors. It's Jip's father. And oh, he is so angry! He is so angry!

Janneke sneaks off home. And Jip is very sad because now he's not going to get a bedtime story when he goes to bed tonight.

But it is partly his own fault. Because books in the bookcase... they're not for cutting up.

Ten red nails
and one red nose

In the bedroom there is a small table. It belongs to
Janneke's mother. And on the table there is a tiny
bottle. That belongs to Janneke's mother too. There
is something in it. Something red.

'What's that?' Jip asks.

'Nail varnish,' Janneke says. 'My mother puts it
on her nails when she's going out. It's beautiful.'

'Does it open?' Jip asks.

'Yes, it opens. See. There's a little brush inside.
Look.' And Janneke shows him. She puts a little bit
of varnish on her fingernail.

'That's pretty,' Jip says. 'Do me too. And this
finger. And the little finger. And now the thumb.'

'My turn again,' says Janneke. It's a fun game and
soon both Jip and Janneke have red nails. They both
have ten red nails.

'There's some left,' Jip says.

'But we've run out of nails,' says Janneke.

'Shall we do Bear's nails too?'

But Bear doesn't have any nails. He's got a nose though. A black nose.

'Would you like a red nose, Bear?'

Bear doesn't say anything. That means he doesn't mind.

And Jip paints Bear's nose red. Red all over. It looks weird. And it's so shiny.

'Can we get it off again?' asks Jip.

'No, never,' says Janneke.

But then Mother comes in. And she laughs and she's angry at the same time. 'You little rascals,' she says. And she takes another bottle and some cotton wool. And she wipes off all the red. She wipes the red off all twenty fingernails. And off Bear's nose.

'There,' says Mother. 'And don't ever touch that bottle again.'

'No, never,' say Jip and Janneke.

Dolly-Dee goes sailing

'Here's an old hat,' says Janneke's mother. 'Go and play with that.'

'Ah!' says Jip.

'Ah!' says Janneke.

But they don't know what to do with the hat. Janneke puts it on. It looks silly.

'It's like a ship,' says Jip.

'A ship should sail,' says Janneke. 'Let's go to the shed. There's a tub of water in there. That's the sea.'

It's great fun. The hat really floats. Just like a boat.

'It needs someone in it,' Janneke says.

'The cat,' says Jip. And he fetches the cat. But the cat doesn't want to go on the ship. The cat is scared. She runs off.

'Dolly-Dee,' says Janneke. 'Dolly-Dee will do it.'

And she's right. Dolly-Dee loves sailing. She sits in the ship in the middle of the sea.

'Here comes a storm,' Jip shouts. And he makes waves with his hands. Great big waves.

'The ship's sinking,' Janneke screams.

And it is. Very slowly, the ship sinks. And poor Dolly-Dee is going down with it.

Whoops! All at once the boat tips over. Dolly-Dee falls in the water.

'Help, help,' Janneke shouts. And she grabs her little girl by the dress. Just in time.

Dolly-Dee is rescued. But wet. Very, very wet. Now she has to put on a new set of dry clothes.

'It was lovely though,' Janneke says. 'Wasn't it, Dolly-Dee?'

Dolly-Dee doesn't say a word. She probably didn't enjoy it that much. But she doesn't let it show.

Saint Nicholas

'Oh, Jip,' Janneke laughs, 'Ha-ha, oh, Jip!'

'What's wrong?' Jip asks.

'You've still got your shoe out,' Janneke says. 'Next to the fire. Just there. And Saint Nicholas has already gone back to Spain.'

Jip turns red. He got so used to putting his shoe out at night. He couldn't stop.

'Saint Nicholas is still here today,' he says. 'You never know, he might bring something.'

'Goodness,' says Jip's mother, 'haven't you had enough presents, Jip? Show Janneke your train.'

It's a very beautiful train. A train with four carriages and real windows.

Janneke got a doll's bath and a little stove. She's brought the doll's bath over with her. But she left the stove at home.

'Are you going to come and have pancakes some time, Jip? I can make real pancakes on my stove.'

'Watch this,' Jip says. 'I'm not Jip, I'm Saint Nicholas.' He goes out of the room and comes back with a long beard.

'Well, well,' he says. 'Have you been a good little girl?'

'Yes, Saint Nicholas,' says Janneke.

'Did you eat your vegetables?' asks the little Saint Nicholas.

'Yes,' says Janneke. 'But you didn't eat yours.'

'Yes, I did,' says Saint Nicholas.

'No, you didn't,' says Janneke. 'I saw it with my

own two eyes. Saint Nicholas didn't eat his
vegetables. Ha-ha.'

'You're a cheeky girl,' Saint Nicholas says. 'You're
going in the sack. Achoo! Achoo!'

Has Saint Nicholas got a cold? No, but the beard
is very itchy. The beard tickles Saint Nicholas's
little nose. He takes the beard off and suddenly it's
Jip again.

And then they play with the train. And when
Dolly-Dee has had enough of riding around on the
train, they give her a bath.

A laughing wolf

'Look, this is the wolf,' Jip says. 'And this is Little Red Riding Hood. It's all in the book.'

'Shall we play Little Red Riding Hood?' asks Janneke. 'You can be the wolf.'

Janneke puts on her red scarf. She takes her mother's shopping basket. Now she looks just like Little Red Riding Hood.

Jip shouts, 'Boo!' But no matter how hard he shouts *boo*, it doesn't turn him into a wolf. He stays Jip.

But he's got an idea! He takes the brown tablecloth. And he wraps it around himself. Then he goes down on all fours. 'Boo!' he shouts. Now Jip is a real wolf.

'Hello, Little Red Riding Hood,' says the wolf.

'Hello, wolf,' says Little Red Riding Hood.

'Where are you going?' asks the wolf.

'I'm going to visit my grandmother,' says Little

Red Riding Hood. 'She's sick. I'm going to take her
a bottle of wine. And a cake. And cigars.'

Now the wolf bursts out laughing. He laughs so
hard he rolls over.

'Cigars!' he shouts. 'Cigars for your grandmother?'

But Janneke is angry. 'Wolves don't laugh,' she
says. 'That's not in the story.'

'All right,' the wolf says. 'I won't laugh. If you go
and pick some flowers, Little Red Riding Hood, I'll
go straight to your grandmother's. Then I'll eat her

up. And then I'll get into her bed. And then you come.'

'Don't tell me what you're going to do,' Janneke shouts. 'You're spoiling it. I'm not supposed to know.'

'Oh,' says Jip, 'you're right. We'll have to start all over again.'

'Hello, Little Red Riding Hood, where are you going?'

'I'm going to Grandmother's, with wine and cigars.'

And again Jip roars with laughter.

And Janneke says, 'I'm not playing anymore.' And she takes off her scarf. And Jip throws off the tablecloth. And they look at the picture instead. The picture of the wolf and Little Red Riding Hood.

Jip the teacher

On Wednesday Jip plays with his train and on Thursday he plays with his train. And then Mother says, 'You got a blackboard too. Aren't you going to play with that?'

'Oh, yes,' Jip says. 'The blackboard. Come on, Janneke. Let's play schools. You're a schoolgirl. Sit down at your desk. I'm the teacher.'

Janneke sits down at her desk like a very good girl.

'What have I written on the board?' asks the teacher.

'Nothing,' says Janneke.

'Yes, I have,' says the teacher. 'What's it say here?'

'It's a little man,' Janneke says. 'A funny little man. Ha-ha, the teacher can't write. The teacher can't write.'

Jip gets angry. 'You're a cheeky little girl,' he says. 'Go and stand in the corner.'

Janneke stands in the corner for ages. And the teacher walks back and forth.

'Is that long enough?' asks Janneke.

'No,' says the teacher. 'You're very naughty. Stay in the corner.'

But the teacher doesn't have anything else to do. There is only one child in the class. And that child is in the corner. That's silly. So the teacher goes and plays with his toy train instead.

'Hey,' Janneke says, 'that's mean.' And now they forget all about school. Dolly-Dee gets to sit on the train. For a very long trip. Where does she go? To Spain. Yes, to Spain. *Toot toot!* There goes the train. Bye-bye, Dolly-Dee.

A snowman
with a broom

'Father,' Jip asks, 'how do you make a snowman?'

'I'll help you,' says Father. He fetches a shovel out of the shed. And he gives Jip a little spade. And Janneke gets one too. And they work very hard.

'It's cold,' Janneke says. 'My hands sting.'

'That will pass,' says Father. 'Keep working.'

Finally the snowman is finished. He is wearing a hat. And he's got a broom. And an orange nose. Because his nose is a carrot.

'Hello,' Janneke says. But the snowman doesn't say a word. If you're made of snow, you don't talk much.

'Mother,' Jip calls, 'come and have a look.'

And Mother comes to have a look. 'What a big white snowman,' she says. 'He's scary. *Eeugh*, you sure he won't bite?'

It makes Janneke laugh. And then she gets on the sled. And Jip has to pull. They go up the hill. Jip has to work very hard. And it's so slippery. *Wham!* He falls over. And the sled goes backwards, really fast. And it pulls Jip along behind, downhill on his stomach.

'Again,' Janneke shouts.

It's so lovely having snow. They spend the whole day sliding down the hill.

But the next morning the snow is gone. The ground is dark again. It's raining.

Jip and Janneke go out to look at the snowman. He's just a pile of slush. And his hat is lying on the ground. And so is his nose. Poor snowman.

An aunty with a car

Aunty Marie is coming today. That's wonderful.
Janneke is putting on her prettiest dress. And Jip
is wearing a new pair of trousers. Because Aunty
Marie is coming in her car. And she's taking Jip
and Janneke out for a drive.

Beep! That's the car!

Jip and Janneke run out.

'I want to go in the front,' Jip shouts.

'No,' Janneke screams. 'I get to go in the front.
It's my aunty.'

That's true. Jip hadn't thought of that. Aunty
Marie is Janneke's aunty.

'You're both going in the back,' Aunty Marie says.
'You have to. But first I'm going to pop inside and
say hello to your mother.'

She seems to take a very long time. But finally, off
they go. With Jip and Janneke in the back.

They're driving! Really fast! The wind whooshes
past. It's lovely.

'We'll stop here for a moment,' Aunty Marie says. And she pulls over.

'Hey, this is the playground,' Jip says.

'Yes, but the playground isn't open yet,' Aunty Marie says. 'It's still winter. We'll just go into the restaurant for a while.'

'Can I have some lemonade?' Janneke shouts.

'And me too?' Jip asks.

'Lemonade in this weather, you'll freeze!' Aunty Marie laughs. But she lets them have some. Aunty Marie never says no. And when their glasses are empty, they're allowed out for a quick go on the seesaw. Even though the playground is closed. Just a quick one.

And then... 'Time to go home,' Aunty Marie calls.

They're back in the car and driving fast and the wind whooshes by. It's so wonderful to have an Aunty Marie. An aunty with a car.

Janneke's birthday party

'I'll just comb your hair,' says Mother. 'You're going to a party! There, now you're a real little gentleman.'

And Jip is the only gentleman at the party. Otherwise there are just two little girls. There are beautiful streamers all over the living room. And Chinese lanterns. And on the table there's a big cake with candles.

Janneke got a new doll and the girls start to play with it. But Jip has had enough of playing with dolls. He wants to play cops and robbers. And the girls don't want to.

Jip gets really angry and grabs Janneke's new doll.

'No!' Janneke screams, 'give it back!'

Janneke's two friends shout, 'You horrible boy.'

And then they hit him. And then they scream as loud as they can and try to kick him.

Janneke's mother rushes in. 'What's going on here?' she says. 'This is supposed to be a party. It's more like the monkey house at the zoo.'

'It's Jip's fault,' Janneke shouts. 'He took my doll.'

'Yes, it's Jip's fault,' the others shout. 'He won't give it back.'

'Now-now,' says Mother, 'we're not here to fight with each other! We're here to enjoy ourselves. Let's play a game. We'll play blind man's buff.'

And that's a lot better. Jip is the blind man first, and then Janneke, and they have lots of fun.

And when Janneke takes off the blindfold, what does she see? Candles. Candles burning on the cake. There are five of them, because Janneke is five years old.

'Who gets to blow out the candles? It's up to you, Janneke,' says Mother. 'Who gets to blow out the candles?'

'Jip,' says Janneke.

And Jip gleams with pride. He blows them out very carefully. All five.

And then they eat some cake.

Too many stamps

'Jip,' says Mother, 'will you pop out to the post office for me? Here's some money. You won't lose it, will you? And here's the letter for Uncle Carl. You have to go up to the counter. And you have to buy ten stamps. And you have to put one stamp on the letter.'

Janneke goes with him. Jip has the letter in one hand. And the money in the other hand.

'Ten stamps, please,' says Jip.

'One, two, three, four... are you watching? Ten!'

'Thank you,' says Jip.

Now he has to put a stamp on the letter. 'I'll do it,' says Janneke. 'I'll lick it.'

Janneke licks the back of the stamp. And she sticks it on the letter. But it ends up crooked. Completely crooked.

'That's no good,' Jip says. 'They won't send a letter off like that.'

'Then we'll put on another one,' Janneke says. 'I'll
lick it.' But uh-oh, the second stamp falls apart, it
goes on in pieces. 'One more,' Jip says. And that's
crooked too. They're starting to enjoy it. They cover
the letter with stamps. Finally it's full. 'Now we'll
post it,' Janneke says. And they put the beautiful
letter in the post box. 'It will get there now,' Jip says.

But when they get home they only have four
stamps. And they've spent all the money. 'What
happened?' asks Mother.

Jip and Janneke tell her what happened. And she gets very angry. 'You two are like little kids,' she says.

And Jip doesn't like that at all. Because he's not a little kid, is he? And Janneke's not either, is she?

Bear falls out
of the plane

Jip has been to the airport with his father. He saw
planes from very close by. 'They're even bigger
than our house,' he tells Janneke. 'They're as big
as from here to the church.'

'They can't be,' Janneke says. 'In the sky they're
just teensy-weensy.'

'It's still true,' Jip says. 'And there are people
inside. And the pilot sits at the front. Shall we play
aeroplanes?'

They line up some chairs. And the piano stool is
the steering wheel. Janneke is a lady who's going
on the plane, and Dolly-Dee and Bear are her
children. Jip gets to be the pilot.

'Will you drive carefully, pilot?' asks the lady.

'Drive?' says the pilot. 'We're not driving, we're
flying.'

'Will you make sure my children don't fall out of the plane?' the lady asks again.

'I'll make sure they don't,' says the pilot. 'And here's a parachute in case they do. Just tie it on.'

Off they go. *Brrr-br-brrr-brrrr...* the plane takes off, up into the sky.

'Oh no,' the lady shouts, 'my children are getting so dizzy.'

'Too late now,' the pilot says. 'We're already a hundred feet up. We're already in Africa.'

'Oh no,' the lady shouts again. 'One of my children just fell out of the window.'

'Did she have a parachute?' the pilot shouts back.

'Yes.'

'Then she's fine. We'll keep going.'

'The other one just fell out of the window as well,' the lady shouts.

'Did he have a parachute?'

'No, we only had one.'

'Then he's dead,' the pilot says.

'Oh, oh!' the lady screams. 'We have to land right away.'

Brrr-brrr-brrr... the plane goes back down to the ground.

What a relief! Both children are alive and kicking, Bear without a parachute and Dolly-Dee with a parachute.

'Goodbye, pilot,' says the lady. 'Thank you very much for the drive.'

'Goodbye, madam,' says the pilot.

Sippy doesn't want to go for a walk

Janneke has a cat.

'What's it called?' Jip asks.

'Sippy,' Janneke says. 'Isn't she cute?'

Yes, Jip thinks Sippy is very cute. But Jip wants to take her outside.

'Hasn't she got a collar?' Jip asks.

'Cats never have collars,' Janneke says.

'We'll tie a piece of string around her neck,' Jip says. 'Then take her for a walk.'

But Sippy doesn't want to go for a walk. Sippy doesn't want a piece of string around her neck either. Sippy is scared. She pulls on one end and Jip and Janneke pull on the other end.

Poor Sippy. Her neck looks so skinny with that string around it.

'You have to!' Jip shouts.

But then Janneke's mother comes in. 'Stop it,' she says. 'Take that string off Sippy's neck. The poor cat. How would you like it if I put a piece of string around your necks. And then pulled it? What would you say? Look, Sippy is crying. Sippy's sad.'

Quickly Janneke unties the string. Sippy creeps off into a corner.

'See?' Mother says. 'Sippy's crying.'

'No, she's not,' Jip says.

What do you think, is Sippy really crying?

Bouncy

There are two sheep in the field. They've got lambs. Two little lambs each. Jip and Janneke go to have a look.

'That one's the cutest,' says Janneke.

'Yes,' Jip says, 'it jumps so high. And it's got such beautiful curls!'

The farmer comes out. 'Hello,' he says. 'They're sweet, aren't they?'

'They're really sweet,' says Jip, 'and that one is the most fun.'

'Okay,' says the farmer. 'That's your lamb then. Give it a name. And play with it.'

Then the farmer goes away. And Janneke says, 'What shall we call it?'

'Pete,' says Jip.

'No,' Janneke says. 'Pete isn't a name for a lamb. We'll call it Bouncy. Because it's just like a bouncy ball of wool.'

'Let's take it home with us,' says Jip.

'Is that allowed?'

'Of course. It's our lamb, isn't it? The farmer said so.'

And together Jip and Janneke pick up the little lamb. It kicks and wriggles. And it calls out, '*Maaaaa!*'

'Come on,' says Jip. 'We'll take you to my mother.' And they take the little lamb home with them.

'What have you got there?' asks Jip's mother.

'This is Bouncy,' Jip says. 'It's ours. The farmer said so.'

'But we can't keep a sheep here,' Mother says. 'What are we supposed to do with it?'

'Oh, please,' Jip and Janneke beg.

'Now listen,' Mother says. 'That lamb wants to go back to its mother. What would you say, Jip, if a big boy came along and carried *you* off? And took you to *his* house? That wouldn't be right, would it? And that lamb's mother is very worried.'

'But it's ours,' Janneke says.

'Yes,' says Mother, 'it's yours. Here's a blue ribbon. Tie it around its neck. And then put it back with its mother. Then the lamb will be happy again. And you'll still know that it's your lamb.'

So the lamb goes back to the field. And it gets to wear a blue ribbon.

'Bye-bye, Bouncy,' says Jip.

'Bye, Bouncy,' says Janneke. 'We'll come back tomorrow.'

'*Maaaa,*' says Bouncy.

A bump
and a bandage

Jip has had a fall. From the top of the piano. That's
very high up. But it was his own fault. Who on
earth climbs on top of a piano? 'I was playing
trucks,' Jip says. 'On top of the piano! And then
I fell off.'

'That's what you get for fooling around,' says
Mother. 'You've got quite a bump.' Yes, Jip's got a
big bump on his head. And a scratch too. And it's
bleeding a little. Jip didn't cry at all. But now that
he's seen the blood, he starts to scream. '*Oo-hoo-
hoo!*' Jip wails. 'Now-now,' says Mother, 'we'll put
a bandage on it. A real bandage.'

Then Janneke comes in. She's a bit shocked.
'What's wrong?' she asks. And then Jip tells her all
about it. 'And I didn't even cry,' he says.

'Yes, you did,' Janneke says, 'I heard you through
the wall.'

'Well, maybe a little bit,' Jip says. 'And I *have* got a bump. Do you want to feel how big it is?'

He lets Janneke feel it. 'I can't feel anything,' she says.

'Here, under the bandage,' Jip says. 'Can't you feel a great big bump right there?'

'Yes,' Janneke says, 'I can feel it.'

Then Jip is very proud. He feels like a hero. Because Janneke is looking at him with awe.

'From the very top of the piano,' Jip says. And he shows her.

All day, Janneke is a little jealous of Jip. And of the big white bandage. 'Maybe you'll fall off the piano too one day,' Jip says.

And that makes her feel a lot better.

Walking through a big puddle

It's raining! It's raining! It's pouring down. And there are big puddles in the street. And water is gushing out of the drainpipes. Everyone is staying inside. Except Jip. Because Jip has a set of waterproofs. And Jip has wellies. It doesn't bother Jip. First he steps over the puddles. Then he walks through them carefully. Then he goes and stands in the middle of a puddle. And he stamps very hard, so that the water splashes up to his ears.

And Janneke? Janneke is sitting at the window. She doesn't have a set of waterproofs. And she doesn't have any wellies. And that's why she's not allowed to go outside. She is very jealous of Jip. Poor Janneke. She watches and she watches. And Jip puts on a show for her. He takes a big run up and jumps right into the middle of the puddle. What a splash!

'Mother,' Janneke asks, 'can't I go out, just for a little while?'

'You'll get wet feet,' says Mother. 'You don't have any wellies.'

Then Janneke's father comes in. He says, 'I've got an idea. You can wear my boots. And then you can go out for a little while with Jip.'

Janneke puts on Father's boots. They're enormous! She can hardly walk. But she goes out anyway and stands next to Jip in the puddle and says, 'Look.'

'Hey,' Jip shouts, 'you look just like Tom Thumb.'

Janneke tries to walk really fast. Like Tom Thumb.

But, oh! Oh no! She's fallen over!

With her nose in the puddle.

And now Janneke is black all over. With mud.

'Jip, inside now,' Jip's mother calls.

'Janneke, inside now,' Janneke's father calls.

The fun is over. Janneke has to have a bath.

'It was just for a little while,' Janneke says, 'but it was still lovely.'

Eggs in the garden

Janneke has a new dress. A green dress. For Easter.

She wants to wear the dress. But Mother says, 'Is that a good idea, Janneke? Trousers are a lot better for playing in.'

'No,' Janneke says. 'I want to wear the dress.'

Fine, Mother lets Janneke wear the dress. She hurries over to show it to Jip.

Jip is in the garden. 'Look, Jip,' she calls out. But what on earth is Jip doing? He's looking for something. In the grass and between the tulips. 'Come on, quick!' he shouts. 'Come on, Janneke. We have to look for eggs. The Easter Bunny has hidden them. Come and help!' Janneke would love to help. But she'd have to get down on her hands and knees. And her dress is brand new.

'I can't,' Janneke says. 'I've got my new dress on.'

'Then I'll look by myself,' Jip says. 'Look, here's

one. See? What a great egg. It's all decorated. If you don't look for them, you won't get any.'

That's too much for Janneke. She doesn't say a word. She runs home.

'What's the matter?' Mother asks.

'Trousers, quick,' Janneke says. And two minutes later, she's back again. In Jip's garden. 'Now I can!' screams Janneke.

'Hurry up then,' Jip says. 'I've already found three. Quick!'

Now they look for eggs together. In the hedge. And between the bushes. And behind the shed. Jip

fetches a basket to put the eggs in. Now he's got four. And Janneke has already got three.

'There should be one more,' Jip says. They search and search. They're both pitch black. From head to toe. It's a good thing Janneke isn't wearing her pretty dress anymore.

'Here it is,' Janneke calls.

'Where?' Jip asks.

'Here, in the chicken coop.' And she's right, the egg is in the chicken coop.

And it really is an egg from the Easter Bunny. And not from a chicken. Because chickens don't lay painted eggs.

'Now we've got four each,' says Jip.

And then they go inside.

A box on wheels

'I'll drive,' Janneke says. 'And you can pull. And
Bear can come too. And so can Dolly-Dee.'

Jip pulls. It goes really well. It's a beautiful cart.
Janneke's father made it. From a box.

'Gee up, horsey,' Janneke says. 'Gee up! Faster.'

Jip pulls as hard as he can, but his legs are so
short. He can't go very fast at all.

'What a lazy horse,' says Janneke. 'Don't you
think he's lazy, Dolly-Dee? Don't you think so,
Bear? We've got a lazy horse.'

Dolly-Dee and Bear agree. But that makes the
horse angry.

'All right then!' the horse shouts. And he pulls
the cart down the hill. And now it goes really fast.
It goes so fast, the horse falls head over heels.

'Help!' Janneke shouts. Then the cart goes bang.
It stops still. But the wheels keep rolling.

Oh no, the wheels have come off.

Jip runs after the wheels. And when he comes back, Janneke is still sitting in the box. With Bear. And with Dolly-Dee. It's not a cart anymore. It's just a box.

'Gee up, horsey,' says Janneke.

'I'm sick of being a horse,' says Jip. 'And the cart's broken! Let's go home.'

That leaves Bear and Dolly-Dee in the cart. A cart without a horse. And without any wheels. Sad, isn't it?

Yes, very sad.

Planting flowers

Jip has his own little garden. He's allowed to dig
it himself. And Janneke helps. Now that they've
dug the garden, Father says, 'I'll help you this
afternoon. We'll plant some flowers. And carrots.
Wait until this afternoon.'

But Jip and Janneke are so impatient. They want
to do something right away. Jip's father has gone to
the office, and Jip says, 'Shall we plant some flowers
ourselves?'

'Okay,' says Janneke. 'How do you plant flowers?'

'I don't know,' Jip says. 'Do you?'

'We've got flowers in our garden,' Janneke says.
'Let's get them.'

So they go to Janneke's house. There are lots of
flowers there. 'We can take these ones,' says
Janneke. And she picks a few flowers.

'And these ones,' says Jip, picking a handful.
Now they've got lots of flowers. And they take them
to Jip's garden.

'Look,' says Jip. 'We dig little holes like this, and then we put in the flowers. And then we close the holes up again.' They work really hard. First they do a row of yellow flowers. Then a row of purple.

'There,' says Janneke. 'Your garden's finished. Hurray!'

When Father comes home, Jip shouts, 'Father, we've already planted the flowers. They're this big.'

'Really?' says Father. 'Show me.'

But when they go to have a look... Oh no, the flowers are already drooping. And some have blown over. It doesn't look beautiful anymore.

It makes Janneke cry. "It was so pretty," she sobs.

'I'm sure it was,' says Father. 'But if you want real flowers in a real garden, you have to plant them properly. You can't just poke them in. Come on, now we'll do it the right way.'

They pull out the flowers. And Father shows them how to plant seeds. Now the garden is all dark-brown earth again. But Father says, 'Just wait, soon it will be green.'

And now they're waiting.

Jip telephones Janneke

'Mother, can I phone Janneke?' Jip asks.

'If you like,' says Mother. 'Shall I dial the number for you?'

'I can do it,' says Jip. And he does it perfectly. He knows the number off by heart.

'Hello,' he says. 'Hello, hello, can I talk to Janneke?'

Then Janneke comes to the phone and says, 'Hello.'

'Hello,' Jip shouts. 'Do you want to come and tell the time on my clock?'

'What?'

'Do you want to come and tell the time on my clock?'

'We've got our own clock,' says Janneke.

'Oh,' says Jip. 'Bye.'

And that's the end of the conversation.

'Mother, Janneke doesn't want to tell the time on my clock,' Jip says.

'Well,' says Mother, 'she probably thinks it's an ordinary clock. Take it over and show her.'

Then Jip goes to Janneke's house.

'I called you on the phone,' he says.

'I know,' Janneke says. 'I talked to you.'

'Here's the clock,' Jip says. 'It's mine. It's a clock for learning how to tell the time. Look. I'll move the hands. What time is it now?'

Janneke doesn't know.

'Eight o'clock, stupid,' says Jip. 'And what time is it now?'

'I don't know.'

But look, Jip doesn't know himself anymore. He doesn't know what time it is on the clock.

Do you?

Two bars
of chocolate

The next-door neighbour has a bucket. A bucket of washing.

'Shall I carry the bucket?' Jip asks.

'No, me,' says Janneke.

'No, me,' says Jip.

'Together,' the neighbour says. 'You can carry the bucket together. To the washing line in my garden.'

Jip and Janneke work hard. It's really heavy. But they are *very* strong! They can manage.

'Phew,' Janneke says. 'We've made it to the washing line. Can we get the washing out of the bucket?'

'If you like,' the neighbour says. 'We can do it together.'

It's a tough job, because there are big sheets in the bucket. 'Leave those sheets to me,' the neighbour says. 'They're too heavy. You can pass me the towels.'

Finally, they're finished. Jip and Janneke are bright red from working so hard.

'Here,' the neighbour says, 'this is for you. Thank you very much.'

She's given them a bar of chocolate each. A big bar of chocolate each.

Jip and Janneke say thank you to the neighbour.

They sit down on the doorstep together. The bars of chocolate really are *very* big. 'Can you eat it all?' Jip asks.

'Yep,' says Janneke. 'Can you?'

'Yep,' says Jip. And they both eat their whole bar of chocolate.

There's Jip's mother at her door. 'Jip, dinner,' she calls.

'I have to go inside,' Jip says. He looks a little pale.

Janneke's mother comes out too. 'Janneke, dinner,' she calls. Janneke goes inside too. She looks very pale.

And did they eat their dinner? I don't think so!

Janneke is missing

'Where's Janneke?' asks Mother. 'Where has Janneke got to?' asks Father.

'Janneke! Janneke!' She's nowhere in sight. Ah, here's Jip. 'Hello, Jip, do you know where Janneke is?'

'No,' says Jip.

Now they start searching. They look in the living room. And in the spare room. And in the bedroom. And in the kitchen. And on the balcony. And in the garden. Mother is so worried. She's almost crying. And Father says, 'Were you playing together, Jip?'

'Yes,' says Jip.

'Where?'

'In the hall,' says Jip. 'We were playing Sleeping Beauty. And Janneke had to sleep for a hundred years. And I was the prince.'

'And where was the castle?'

'In the cupboard,' says Jip.

Then Father opens the cupboard. And there she is. Sleeping Beauty. Asleep with her head on the vacuum cleaner. And her arms around the mop.

Father gives her a little shake and wakes her up. And Mother is so happy she kisses her.

But Janneke is totally confused. 'I was Sleeping Beauty,' she says. 'But then I fell asleep for real.'

Mother laughs. But Jip doesn't look so happy.

'What's wrong, Jip?'

'I was the prince,' Jip says. 'I was supposed to wake her up in a hundred years. But I forgot. I went outside to play.'

'What a terrible prince,' says Father.

And then they go into the living room. For a glass of lemonade to calm their nerves.

Janneke comes to stay

Jip is playing in the garden. He shouts over the hedge, 'Janneke!'

Where has Janneke got to? He hasn't seen her all day.

Again, Jip calls out, 'Janneke!'

And then Janneke comes out of her back door. She is carrying a suitcase. And she's wearing her hat. And she struts over to the hedge.

'What are you doing?' Jip asks with surprise.

'I'm staying the night,' says Janneke.

'You're staying the night? Where?'

'At your house,' says Janneke and she crawls through the hole in the hedge. Holding her suitcase and with her hat on her head, she crawls through the hole in the hedge. It looks ridiculous. Jip roars with laughter. But he doesn't understand.

'My mother and father are going away,' Janneke says. 'Until the day after tomorrow. And I'm allowed to stay at your house. That's what this suitcase is for.'

'What's in it?' Jip asks.

'A nightie. And a toothbrush. And toothpaste. And Dolly-Dee. And something else. A surprise.'

'Are you going to sleep in the guest room?'

'I don't know,' Janneke says. 'Shall we ask?'

They go inside together.

'Ah,' says Jip's mother. 'Our guest has arrived. Hello. Jip, will you show our guest to her room. And help her unpack her suitcase.'

'Look,' Jip says. 'You sleep here. In this bed. Now show me the surprise.'

Janneke opens the suitcase. On top of everything else there is a big piece of chocolate. 'That's for you,' Janneke says.

And that evening they get to brush their teeth together. And wash their faces together. And listen to the bedtime story together. With Jip in his pyjamas. And Janneke in her nightie. Jip's father tells them the story. About three little pigs. And when it's finished, he tells it again. And when it's finished, again.

'And now to bed,' says Mother. 'Do you know what time it is? It's eight o'clock. Long past your bedtime!'

But it's not every day that Janneke comes to stay the night.

94

The shoemaker

'There's a hole in my shoe,' Jip says. 'My foot is wet.'

'Well,' says Mother, 'hurry off to the shoemaker's then. You can go together. No, not just one shoe. Take both of them.'

'Only one of them's got a hole,' says Jip.

'The other one's starting to go too,' says Mother. 'Heels and soles, that's what you need to say.'

Jip says, 'Heels and soles,' to the shoemaker.

Janneke says, 'Heels and soles,' too.

'Dear oh dear,' says the shoemaker. 'You've been walking too much, Jip. You're in trouble again. You'll have to start walking on your hands. Then you won't wear out so many shoes.'

Tap, tap, goes the hammer. *Tick, tick, rata-tatta-tat.*

The shoemaker has so much work to do.

'There must be a thousand shoes here,' says Janneke.

'More than that,' says Jip. 'Hundreds.'

'Yes,' the shoemaker says. 'It's not your turn just yet. You'll have to wait a good week. You'll have to walk around barefoot, Jip.'

'No, I don't,' Jip says. 'I've got two other pairs. And I've still got my wellies.'

'Look at me,' Janneke calls.

Jip and the shoemaker look at Janneke. She's

standing there with two big shoes on. Shoes with high heels.

'Look at that,' the shoemaker says. 'You're a lady now. Good morning, madam. Are you going shopping?'

'Yes,' the lady answers, walking very primly across the floor. But *thud*, she falls on her nose.

'Serves you right,' says Jip. 'Coming?' And he says goodbye to the shoemaker.

'Bye, Jip,' the shoemaker says. 'And goodbye, madam.'

'Goodbye, shoemaker,' says Janneke.

A nest with eggs

'Come and have a look! Come and have a look!' Jip
shouts.

He shouts so loud that everyone comes running.

Janneke screams, 'What is it?'

'A nest!' Jip shouts. 'A nest with eggs. Here in the
tree!'

Together they climb up onto the lowest branch
of the tree. And sure enough. There they are. Six
beautiful light-blue eggs in a nest.

'Ooh,' says Janneke, 'they're so pretty. Little birds
are going to hatch out of them.'

'It will be all right if I take one, won't it?' says Jip,
reaching out a hand.

'No,' Janneke says. 'When the mother bird comes
back she'll notice.'

'Mother birds can't count,' says Jip.

But who's coming now? Not the mother bird, but
Jip's mother. 'Come on,' she says. 'That's enough.
Come away now.'

'Why?' asks Janneke. 'We're not doing anything.'

'Just come away,' says Mother. 'We'll sit down over there on the bench.'

When they're sitting on the bench, she says, 'You should never shout and scream next to a bird's nest. That's not right. And going and looking too often isn't right either. The mother bird will get scared. And then she won't come back.'

'What about when the little birds are there?' Jip asks. 'Can we go and have a look then?'

'No,' says Mother. 'You have to leave them in peace. Birds are scared of us. Imagine you were sitting in a nest and an elephant came to look at you. You'd be frightened too, wouldn't you? But look, the mother bird has come back. You're not going to be noisy now, are you?'

Jip and Janneke promise to keep quiet.

And two days later, when the chicks have hatched out of the eggs, Jip and Janneke are allowed to go for one quick look. With Father. Just for a moment.

'We're elephants now,' Janneke says.

'That's right,' says Father. 'And now we'll leave them alone. Bye-bye, birdies.'

A kangaroo
in the porridge oats

'Mother,' Jip calls.

'What?'

'Can I buy a box of porridge oats?'

'Again?' says Mother. 'The tin's already full.'

'Oh, please,' Jip says. 'I really want a kangaroo.'

Mother laughs. There's a picture in every box of porridge oats. And Jip and Janneke collect the pictures. They're pictures of animals. Jip and Janneke have already got a chimp and an elephant and a zebra and lots more, and they've stuck them all in an album. But they're missing a kangaroo.

'All right, then,' Mother says. 'Go and buy a box of oats. And take Janneke with you.' Together they go to the shop.

'One box of porridge oats, please,' says Jip. 'With a picture. And it has to be a kangaroo.'

'I can't tell what it is,' says the lady in the shop.
'The picture's inside the box. You have to wait and
see.'

Jip and Janneke run all the way home.

'Let's have a look,' says Jip. 'It's bound to be a
kangaroo this time.'

But when they open the box the picture falls out.
It's another chimp.

Jip is angry. 'Not another chimp,' he shouts. 'I've already got a chimp. Mother, can I buy another box of porridge?'

'No,' says Mother. 'I've got enough now to make porridge every day for six weeks. If you eat a whole mixing bowl full of porridge between the two of you tomorrow, then I don't mind. How would that be? Janneke, will you come over tomorrow morning to eat a mixing bowl full of porridge, together with Jip?'

'No,' Janneke says. 'I have enough trouble with a normal bowl.'

'Now I'm stuck with two chimps!' bellows Jip.

'You should try to swap,' says Mother. 'Swap it with your friends in the street.'

That's an idea. Jip stays out on the street all afternoon to swap one of his chimps. But not one of the other boys eats porridge at home.

When Jip comes back with his head hanging, Janneke is at the door. 'Look,' she says.

'A kangaroo!' Jip shouts.

'Yep,' Janneke says. 'My mother let me buy a box of porridge oats. And it was inside.'

'Great,' says Jip. 'Let's stick it in the book right away.'

Paddling

'Look,' says Jip, 'those boys are paddling.'

'Yes,' Janneke says. 'But they're big boys.'

'Let's join in,' Jip says. 'We're big too.'

He takes off his shoes.

'Is it allowed?' asks Janneke.

'Of course it is,' Jip says. 'Come on, take off your shoes, Janneke.'

Janneke thinks it's a bit yucky. But she takes her shoes off anyway.

'It's not too deep?' she asks.

'No, it's great,' Jip says. He's already up to his ankles in the water. 'Just a bit muddy.'

'Are there any creepy-crawlies in the water?' Janneke asks.

'No,' Jip says, 'come on in.'

Then Janneke goes in too. It's fun. The water is cold, but they don't mind.

But the big boys aren't nice. They tease Jip and

Janneke. And splash them. 'Stop it,' Jip screams. But they do it anyway. And they bump Janneke and try to push her over.

Finally the big boys go away.

'See,' Jip says. 'I chased them off.' And he is proud of himself.

But now it's no fun anymore.

Sopping wet and covered with mud, Jip and Janneke clamber up onto dry land.

'Where are my shoes?' exclaims Janneke.

The shoes are gone. Oh no, the big boys have taken them.

'There!' Jip shouts.

Janneke's shoes are dangling from a tree. Very high up.

'I'll never reach them,' says Janneke.

'I know,' says Jip, 'climb up onto my shoulders, then you'll reach.'

And that's what they do. And it works. Up on Jip's shoulders, Janneke can just reach the shoes.

Phew, what a relief. They are so happy.

But Jip's mother is not happy. And Janneke's mother is not happy either. Because when the two of them get home they have to go straight into the bath. And so do their clothes.

Jip fights with a billy goat

'Come quick, come quick,' Jip shouts. 'I just saw a billy goat.'

'Where?' asks Janneke.

'Out on the road,' Jip says.

And he's right, there's the billy goat. It's loose. It's run away. It's a naughty little billy goat.

'I'll take you back home,' says Jip. And he grabs the goat.

'Don't,' Janneke shouts. 'It will bump you with its horns.'

'I'm not scared,' says Jip.

But the goat doesn't want to go with him. It jumps in the air. It turns to face Jip. And then it starts. It butts Jip with its horns.

'Careful,' Janneke screams.

But Jip isn't scared at all. He butts back. Now

there are two little billy goats.

'Ow,' Jip shouts. 'Stupid goat. That hurts!'

But the goat doesn't care. It keeps butting him. And it does it really hard. Jip falls over.

'Just wait,' Janneke says bravely. 'Just wait.' She takes off her socks. And she goes over to the little billy goat. 'Boo!' she shouts at the top of her voice. The goat stands still for a moment. It looks surprised. It thinks, *Who's that shouting boo?* And while it's standing there, Janneke puts her socks on the goat. Not on its feet. No, on its horns.

'There,' Janneke says. 'Now bump away.'

Jip is already standing up waiting. And now he goes back to fighting the goat. The little billy goat butts its head – *boom, bang* – against Jip's. But it doesn't hurt anymore. Because the billy goat has socks on.

And then the farmer comes up.

'There you are, you naughty goat,' he says. 'You're coming back with me.' And he leads the billy goat away. On a rope.

'My socks,' Janneke shouts. 'He's got my socks on!'

'Oh,' the farmer says, 'I thought you'd given them to him as a present.'

'No,' Janneke shouts angrily.

Then she gets her socks back. But the billy goat looks sad. Is it because he's tied up again? Or because he's lost his pretty socks?

Jip sings
in the street

'Mother,' Jip calls, 'there's a man out on the street. He's singing.'

'I can hear him,' says Mother. 'Here, take some money out to him. He's earned it.'

Jip gives the man the money and then goes over to Janneke's.

'You coming to earn some money?' he asks. 'By singing in the street?'

'Can you earn money doing that?' asks Janneke.

'Yep. I'll do the singing, you bring your father's big hat.'

There they are in the lane. Jip sings as loud as he can. It makes him go hoarse. And Janneke stands there with the hat. But no one gives them anything. No one pays any attention.

'You have to ask,' Jip says. 'Here comes a lady.

Ask her for some money for the singer.'

Janneke feels very shy. But she does it anyway.

'Goodness,' says the lady. 'Are you collecting? Here you are then,' and she gives Janneke two coins.

But nobody else comes along.

'I'm stopping,' Jip says. 'I can't go on. I've lost my voice.'

'Look, Mother, we've made some money,' Jip says when they get back home.

'How?' asks Mother.

'By singing,' Jip says. 'Like that man before.'

'Oh,' says Mother, 'you mustn't do that. You can sing, but not for money.'

'But we made good money,' Jip says.

'Tomorrow we'll give that money to the man who sings on the street,' says Mother. 'And I'll give you some shortbread now, if you sing a little bit more for me.'

Jip and Janneke sing a song for her. And they both get a big piece of shortbread.

Jip hoses
down poor kitty

It is so hot! It is so *verrrrry* hot! Janneke doesn't
want to play anymore. She's lying on the lawn. In
just her swimming costume.

'Wait,' says Jip. 'I'll hose you down.'

'No,' Janneke screams.

'Yes,' Jip says. 'Yes, yes, I'm going to make you all
wet.'

And Jip grabs the hose. He turns on the tap.
Janneke runs away as fast as she can. But it doesn't
help. She gets a big spray of water all over her.

'Hey! Hey!!' roars Janneke. 'Stop it!'

But Jip doesn't stop until Janneke is sop-sop-
sopping. And actually it's lovely. Suddenly she's
nice and cool.

'Now you!' she says. And she grabs the hose.

'No! I don't want to!' Jip cries. He really is scared.

But Janneke is not about to feel sorry for him. And she hits Jip with such a big blast of water that his hair is dripping. There's a whole puddle around him. Now they are both wet. And they're both nice and cool.

'And now the cat,' says Jip.

'You're not allowed to make cats wet,' says Janneke. 'That's mean. Sippy hates it.'

'Aw, come on, just a little bit,' Jip whines. And he runs after kitty. And he catches the poor cat with a big squirt. She cries *meow* at the top of her voice and suddenly she's gone. There she is. Up the tree. And very wet.

'Nasty boy,' says Janneke.

'She'll dry off again,' Jip says. 'In the sun.'

And kitty does dry off again. But she stays angry at Jip for three whole days. And hisses at him. And that's just what he deserves.

An uncle
with a beard

'I've got an uncle,' says Janneke.

'So what?' says Jip. 'I've got four. Four uncles!'

'Yes, but I've got an uncle with a beard,' says Janneke.

Jip can't beat that.

'Where is he?' asks Jip.

'At our house,' says Janneke. 'Do you want to come and have a look?'

'Yes,' says Jip. He's never seen an uncle with a beard before.

The uncle is at Janneke's house. Sitting on the sofa. And his beard is really long. Jip thinks it's a bit scary.

'Are you Jip?' asks the uncle. 'Come over here, I'm Uncle Paul.'

Jip moves closer very slowly. He's actually afraid

of the beard. But he doesn't want to let it show. Because then Janneke would think he's chicken. And Jip's not chicken. 'Hello, sir,' says Jip.

'Call me Uncle Paul.'

'Hello, Uncle Paul,' Jip whispers.

'Would you like to come and sit on my knee, Jip?'

But Jip definitely doesn't dare to do that. He turns red and stays where he is. A long way from Uncle Paul.

'I will,' says Janneke, and *zoom*, there she is, on her uncle's knee. And she even pulls his beard. 'Story!' she shouts. 'Tell us a story. About the prince and the princess.'

Now Uncle Paul tells them a story. A really wonderful story. And Jip inches closer. And suddenly there he is, sitting on Uncle Paul's other knee. Just like that. From up close the beard isn't scary at all. But it does tickle Jip's nose.

'Achoo!' says Jip.

'And then...' Uncle Paul says, 'then the prince married the princess and they lived happily ever after.'

'Is that the end, Uncle Paul?'

'That's the end.'

'Really?' moans Janneke.

'Okay,' says Uncle Paul. 'There's more. Then they heard the ice-cream van. And the prince and the princess went out and bought ice creams.'

'I can hear the ice-cream van too,' says Janneke.

'Then this prince and princess can go and buy ice creams too,' says Uncle Paul. 'Off you go, off my knees, and here's some money for two ice creams.'

When Jip gets home, he says, 'Mother, why haven't I got an uncle with a beard?'

'I don't know,' laughs Mother.

'I want an uncle with a beard,' says Jip.

'Fine,' says Mother. 'I'll buy you one.'

They come home with a dog

'Janneke,' says Mother, 'you know Smit's? The shop with material and wool?'

'Yes,' says Janneke.

'Could you go there and get me a packet of needles? Fine needles, not thick ones.'

'Okay,' says Janneke. And she calls Jip. 'You coming to buy needles?'

Off they go together. It's a nice day. There are lots of things to see out on the street. There is a woman with flowers. And a cart with plums. The plum man gives Jip and Janneke a plum each to eat.

'Look, that dog's following us,' says Jip.

'You're right,' says Janneke, 'what a funny little dog. A funny, long dog. Its back legs are miles away from its front legs.'

'It's dirty,' says Jip. 'But it's cute.'

'Go back to your master,' Janneke says, 'go back now.'

But the dog doesn't want to go back. It wants to follow them.

'Poor little dog,' says Janneke, 'don't you have a master?'

The dog gives her a sorrowful look.

'Don't you have a home?'

The dog can't talk, but its eyes say, 'No, I don't have a home.'

'You can come with us then,' says Janneke.

'That's right,' Jip says. 'You can live at my house.'

'No, at my house,' says Janneke.

'No, at my house,' Jip shouts.

Now they start to argue. And they forget all about the needles. And they go back to Janneke's mother in a very bad mood with the dog following along behind.

'What's all this about?' asks Mother. 'Where are the needles? And what's that filthy animal doing here?'

'It's not a filthy animal,' Jip shouts. 'It's my dog!'

'No, it's not,' screams Janneke, 'It's *my* dog.'

Then Jip's mother comes out as well. And finally the dog gets to go in the tub at Jip's house. And after it's clean, they let it sleep in a basket at Janneke's.

And it gets a food bowl at Jip's.

And a food bowl at Janneke's.

Now the dog belongs to both of them.

And what's it called? It's called Weenie.

And the mothers say, 'Oh, these children! You send them out for needles and they come back with a dog.'

Weenie is a good boy

'Weenie,' asks Jip, 'who do you love the most, me or Janneke? Tell us who you love, Weenie.'

'Woof,' says Weenie.

'Do you love me more?' asks Janneke.

'Woof,' says Weenie.

That's no help at all. What is *woof* supposed to mean?

'I know,' says Jip, 'I'll walk this way. And you walk that way, Janneke. And then we'll see who Weenie follows.

'Okay,' says Janneke. 'But you're not allowed to call him.'

They both walk in opposite directions. And Weenie?

Weenie stays sitting there. First he looks at Jip and then he looks at Janneke. He keeps looking from one to the other. But he stays sitting there and whimpers a little.

'He loves us both just as much,' says Janneke. 'See?' And she's right.

Weenie is a very sweet little dog. But he is so scared of the cat. He keeps forgetting that they have a cat as well. He keeps scampering into Janneke's house to eat out of his bowl. And then he hears *Tsssss!* That's the cat. She's standing there with a

bristling tail. And hissing as loud as she can. She's very angry at Weenie. That gives Weenie such a fright that he runs off. With his tail between his legs.

'Oh, come here,' says Janneke, lifting him up onto her lap. 'You're a real scaredy-cat. You're not a brave doggy at all, Weenie.'

But Weenie is still so little. And the cat's tail looks so big.

'They'll get used to each other,' says Janneke's mother. 'In a while they'll be sleeping together in the same basket.'

'*Tsssss*,' hisses the cat. As if to say, 'In the same basket? Not if I have anything to do with it!'

Jip cuts himself

'You coming? I'm going to play outside,' says Jip.

'Not now,' Janneke says. 'I have to peel some apples. A whole bucket full of apples. We're going to stew them.'

'I can peel apples too,' says Jip.

'I've only got one knife,' says Janneke.

'I'll go and get one.' Jip runs home to fetch a knife. From the kitchen. And he runs back to Janneke's with the knife.

Now he's ready to peel some apples.

'Look,' says Janneke. 'I can make really long, wriggly peels. It's really hard. But I can do it.'

Jip does his best. He tries so hard he turns red. But the peel breaks off.

'You have to do it like this,' Janneke says. 'Look, like this.'

Jip does it like that. But... Oh! Gee! Ow! He's cut his thumb.

Blood comes out. What a shock!

Jip stands there holding his thumb up in the air and looking very frightened.

'Mother!' Janneke calls. Her mother comes running.

'What is it?' she calls, but she's already seen what it is.

'Hang on,' she says. 'Let me wrap that thumb up for you. I've got a nice bandage for it. Come with me. Does it hurt?'

'Yes,' says Jip. 'But I'm not crying.'

No, Jip is very brave and he's not crying. Janneke's mother wraps a rag around his thumb and Janneke watches.

'He wanted to peel some apples,' she tells her mother. 'And then he went home to get a knife.'

'Yes, I can see that,' her mother says. 'But that knife is very sharp. Much too sharp. From now on, ask first, Jip, if you want a knife. And you know what we'll do now? Janneke can peel and Jip can eat. Seeing as Jip is wounded, he can eat some apple.'

And that's much better. Because peeling is difficult. But eating is easy.

Weenie
carries everything

'Here,' says the farmer's wife. 'I've got four eggs for you. Two each. You can take them home for breakfast.'

She gives Jip two eggs and she gives Janneke two eggs.

'Thank you,' say Jip and Janneke.

'Wait a second,' says the farmer's wife. 'I've got a little basket too. An Easter egg basket. You can have it.'

Jip and Janneke put the eggs in the basket. And then they set off home.

Jip says, 'It's Weenie's job to carry the basket. He can manage that.'

'Yes,' says Janneke, 'he can manage that. He always carries the newspaper. He brings it in.'

'Weenie,' Jip calls. 'There's a good boy. Good boy.

Here, carry this for your master. Hold it in your mouth like a good boy.'

And Weenie is a very smart dog. He understands. He carries the basket very carefully.

'See,' Janneke says, 'he can do it. We'll never have to carry anything again. Weenie can do it for us.'

They're almost home.

And then suddenly something happens. A bird flies very low over the road. A flapping bird. 'Woof, woof!' shouts Weenie. And he runs after the bird.

Oh no! Weenie's dropped the basket. And the four eggs have rolled out. Two are smashed. And two are still whole. And the basket is sticky and wet and yellow.

'Weenie!' Jip screams. 'Weenie!! Come here at once.'

Weenie turns around. The bird has flown off. And Weenie comes up to Jip very slowly. He's holding his tail between his legs. He is a sad little dog.

'Bad dog,' says Janneke.

'Bad dog,' says Jip.

Poor Weenie wags his tail. He understands. He knows perfectly well that he's been naughty. And that he shouldn't have dropped the basket like that. But he's such a little dog.

At home Jip's mother says, 'Give it to me, I'll clean the basket. And you've still got one egg each. You can't blame Weenie. Weenie can carry the newspaper. But he can't carry eggs.'

They know that now.

Plasticine people

There's a thunderstorm. Jip and Janneke are in the living room. *Boom! Bang! Ba-ba-ba-boom!* say the clouds. And then after a while the sky lights up, *flash!* And then there's another *ba-ba-ba-boom!*

'I'm not frightened,' says Jip.

'I'm not frightened either,' says Janneke. But her voice is quivering. She gets down on the floor and sticks her head under the table.

'What are you doing?' asks Jip.

'Nothing,' Janneke says. 'I'm looking for something.' But she's not really looking for something. She's just scared.

'I know,' says Mother. 'We'll do some modelling. We'll make people and animals. From plasticine. And there's a waffle for whoever makes the best figure.' She gets out the box of plasticine and they set to work.

Jip makes a whole family. He makes a plasticine

father, a plasticine mother, and seven little children, all made of plasticine.

Janneke is working on an animal.

'What kind of animal is it, Janneke?'

But Janneke doesn't want to say. She works very hard. *Boom, boom, ba-ba-boom*, say the clouds. But Janneke is so busy she doesn't even hear it.

'Finished,' Jip shouts.

'Oh, beautiful,' says Mother. 'It's a shame the children don't have any legs. And they don't have any heads either. But otherwise they're beautiful.'

'I've finished too,' Janneke says.

'Is it an elephant?' asks Jip.

'No!' says Janneke. 'It's a dog. You can see that, can't you?'

'Of course, I can,' says Mother. 'It's a dog. I can see that. It's Weenie.'

'Who wins,' Jip shouts. 'Have I won?'

Mother looks again and says, 'Janneke wins. Her dog has legs and it's got a head. But Jip's people are lovely too. And that's why you both get a waffle. And just look outside!'

They look out of the window. Outside the sun is shining. The thunderstorm is over.

'Here,' says Mother. 'A big waffle each.'

And they go outside to eat them.

Weenie
comes to dinner

'Jip, what are you making such a fuss about?' asks
Mother. 'You're taking an hour to eat a sandwich.
And Janneke is already here for you. You'll have to
wait a minute, Janneke. Jip's still eating. Would you
like a sandwich too?'

'Yes, please,' says Janneke.

They sit eating together. It's nice. But Jip still
dawdles.

'Let's play dinner parties,' says Janneke. 'And
we've got a guest. Weenie is the guest. He's come
to dinner.'

'Okay,' says Jip. He ties a serviette around
Weenie's neck. And he puts Weenie on a chair.
Weenie is a very nice guest. He sits there like a good
boy and looks around.

'Would you like a sandwich?' Janneke asks the
guest.

Weenie doesn't say a thing.

'A jam sandwich?' asks Jip.

Now Weenie looks interested.

'Or would you prefer honey?' asks Janneke.

But uh-oh, suddenly the guest jumps up. He jumps onto the table. He grabs a sandwich and jumps off the table and runs through the room.

'Hey! Stop!' shouts Jip.

Mother takes the sandwich from Weenie. She laughs and says, 'Your guest isn't very polite. I think you need to invite someone else to your dinner party. But first Jip gets another sandwich. And three minutes to eat it up.'

And Jip eats the whole sandwich in four minutes.

And that's fast too.

Weenie is gone

It's so sad. It's terrible! Weenie is gone. Weenie has run away. He's been missing since this morning. Jip called, 'Weenie!' And Janneke called, 'Wee-wee-wee-weenie!'

But he didn't come back. And now it's evening and Weenie still hasn't come back.

'I'm not going to bed,' says Jip.

'You can't stay up all night,' says Mother. 'Tomorrow we'll go to the police station. And we'll ask them if they've found Weenie.'

And a very sad Jip goes to brush his teeth. He has to go to sleep and meanwhile Weenie could be completely lost, somewhere far away.

'I'll come and tuck you in,' says Father. 'Don't worry, Jip. Tomorrow we'll go to the police station. It will be all right.' But after Father has gone away, Jip has a little cry. And then he falls asleep.

And in the middle of the night Jip wakes up.

What's that noise? He hears quiet whimpering. Jip is out of bed in a flash. Weenie!

He hurries downstairs and carefully opens the back door. Weenie rushes in. He's whining with happiness. He jumps up on Jip. He licks Jip on the nose. 'Oh, Weenie,' Jip says. 'Where were you? Did a bad man take you away? Or did you get lost? Where were you?'

But Weenie can't tell Jip where he was.

Jip and Weenie roll around the hall together and have a great time.

Then suddenly someone is on the stairs. It's Mother.

'What's that noise?' she asks, startled. 'What's going on? Are you downstairs, Jip?'

'Weenie's come back,' Jip yells. "Weenie's back. Can I go and tell Janneke?'

'No,' says Mother. 'It's the middle of the night. Hurry up and get back into bed. Janneke will see for herself tomorrow.'

And just for once Weenie is allowed to sleep in Jip's room. On the rug next to his bed.

Weenie in the ditch

'Put on your scarf,' says Mother. 'Put on your new red scarf, Jip. And you too, Janneke. Have you got your pretty new scarf on? The green one? Good. Don't go too far away now!'

Jip and Janneke go out onto the street with Weenie. They walk very quickly because it's cold. And Weenie leads the way. Janneke throws a stone. And Weenie runs after it. He picks the stone up in his mouth and brings it back like a good dog.

Jip throws another stone. Much further away. And Weenie is so happy he almost goes crazy.

'Woof, woof,' he says and brings back all the stones.

Then Jip throws a stick in the ditch.

'No, don't!' Janneke says. 'Careful!'

But it's too late. Weenie jumps, splash, into the filthy ditch. He whines and pants. Oh, oh, it's so cold! 'He's drowning,' Janneke wails.

'He'll catch cold,' Jip screams.

But Weenie doesn't drown. He's a good swimmer and paddles back to the side of the ditch with the stick in his mouth.

'We have to dry him off,' says Jip. 'Otherwise he'll get sick. And he takes his new scarf and uses it to dry Weenie. And Janneke takes her pretty green scarf. And she helps.

Now Weenie is almost dry. He gives a cheerful bark and races around to warm up.

But the scarves are so dirty. So dirty. From all the mud.

'Look at you,' says Mother when they get home.

'We had to dry Weenie,' Jip says. 'To keep him warm.'

'I'll warm your bottoms,' says Mother in an angry voice.

But Jip can see that she's secretly smiling.

Jip and Janneke
get married

'When I grow up,' Jip says, 'I'm going to be a pilot. What do you want to be when you grow up?'

'I want to be a mother,' says Janneke.

'Then you'll have to get married first,' says Jip.

'I will,' Janneke says. 'I'm going to get married.'

'To a pilot?' asks Jip.

'Yes,' says Janneke. 'A pilot would be all right.'

'Then you can marry me,' Jip says. 'Do you want to come and get married?'

'How?' asks Janneke.

'You know. In church. The shed is the church. And you have to wear a veil. A long one. And I have to put on a hat.'

Here come the bride and groom. Arm in arm to the church. But there's no minister in the church. What are they supposed to do about that?

'Bear is the minister,' Jip says. And the stepladder is the pulpit. They wrap a black cloth around Bear.

'I think that's everything,' Jip says. And then Jip's mother comes into the shed and says, 'May I congratulate the happy couple? The wedding banquet is ready. Two currant buns each.'

'I don't want anything to eat,' Jip shouts. 'I want to finally get to be a pilot.'

'You have to eat,' Janneke says. 'That's part of weddings.' And she pulls him along behind her.

'No,' Jip screams, giving Janneke a whack.

'Shame on you,' says Mother. 'Hitting your wife! When you've only just got married. What a scandal!'

Janneke thinks so too. But look, the bridegroom is sorry. And that's a good start.

And then they go and eat.

Who can eat
the most pancakes?

'Hey, pancakes,' says Jip.

'Great, pancakes,' says Janneke.

'Mmm, pancakes,' says Jip's father.

And Jip's mother is at the stove. With a red face. She gives them pancakes in turn.

'Shall we see who can eat the most pancakes?' asks Father.

'Yes!' shouts Jip.

'Yes,' says Janneke. 'What does the winner get?'

'A pancake,' says Father.

'Now now,' says Mother, 'that's no fun. No, whoever eats the most pancakes gets a medal.'

Jip has already had three pancakes.

And Father has only had one.

Now they start to eat really fast. As fast as they can. Finally, Father says, 'I can't eat any more.'

'How many have you had?' asks Mother.

'Three.'

And after a while Jip says, 'I can't eat any more either.'

'How many have *you* had?'

'Four,' says Jip.

And just look at Janneke. She doesn't stop eating. She eats and eats. 'How many have you had, Janneke?'

'Five,' sighs Janneke.

'Well done,' says Mother. 'You get the medal.' And she makes a gold medal for Janneke. A pancake medal on a red ribbon. She pins it to Janneke's dress. And Janneke is so proud. She is *so* proud. And Jip? What do you think? Jip really is a little bit jealous.

Jip is a girl

'I have to get some rice,' Janneke says. 'And margarine. At the shop. Do you want to come, Jip?'

'All right,' Jip says. He slips his coat on and walks straight out the door.

'What do you think you're doing?' calls Mother. 'Put your hat on this instant. Going out in the cold without a hat. You can't do that.'

But Jip doesn't want to wear his hat.

'I want a scarf over my head, like Janneke.'

Because Janneke has a pretty scarf wrapped around her head. With red and yellow stripes. And knotted at the top.

'Well,' says Mother, 'if that's what you want, it's fine by me. Come here.' And she wraps a scarf around Jip's head. A green checked scarf. With a knot at the top.

'There, now you're both wrapped up nice and warm.'

The shopkeeper is called Mr Dekker.

He has lots of jars on the counter. With liquorice. And boiled sweets. And aniseed balls. Mr Dekker always gives something to Jip and Janneke.

'Hello, Mr Dekker,' says Janneke.

'Hello, girls,' says Mr Dekker.

Jip turns bright red. *Girls!*

'I'm not a girl,' he snaps. 'I'm a boy!'

'Oh,' says Mr Dekker. 'Oh, I didn't notice.'

'But I've got trousers on,' says Jip.

'True,' says Mr Dekker, 'but so has this little girl.' And he's right. Janneke always wears trousers when it's cold.

'And you're both wearing girl's hats,' says Mr Dekker.

Jip pulls the scarf off his head straightaway.

'Oh, now I see,' says Mr Dekker. 'Hello, little boy.'

Then Janneke buys some rice and margarine and Mr Dekker gives them both a large toffee.

When they get home Jip is still angry. 'Girls!' he growls.

'Well,' says Mother, 'you asked for it.'

The most famous twentieth-century Dutch writer, ANNIE M.G. SCHMIDT (1911 – 1995) was thought of during her lifetime as the 'real queen of the Netherlands'. She was a highly original woman with a broad perspective and an unfailing sense of humour. Her radio and TV series, plays and musicals brought her unprecedented popularity. Many of her books have been filmed, and almost everyone in the Netherlands is able to recite at least a line or two from one of her songs or poems. Her children's books have become a national institution.

Throughout her career – she died in 1995 at the age of 84 – she was showered with accolades. In 1988 the Swedish author Astrid Lindgren presented her with the Hans Christian Andersen Award, the 'Nobel Prize' of children's literature. The jury praised her 'ironic tone, witty criticism and style that is amusing, clear, rebellious and simple to its essence.'

FIEP WESTENDORP (1916 – 2004) established her name in the fifties with the black-and-white drawings she did to accompany the Jip and Janneke stories in the national daily *Het Parool*. To make the pictures stand out in the newspaper, Fiep drew the duo in silhouette, and this style worked so well that she maintained it through all of her Jip and Janneke illustrations. Now, more than fifty years later, there is not a child in the Netherlands who does not immediately recognise the characters. Although her illustrations for other famous authors were also very successful, Fiep Westendorp preferred to work with Annie M.G. Schmidt. Their senses of humour in particular were a perfect match.

In 1997 Fiep Westendorp was awarded the 'Oeuvre Paintbrush', a prize that was specially created to honour her entire oeuvre.